actually a mitt, is larger than most. Why is this? The larger mitt gives the first baseman more surface area to catch the ball. This is useful for the many times when ground balls are hit to other infielders, and they have to throw quickly to first base. The larger mitt helps first basemen capture balls that aren't thrown perfectly.

Fast Fact

There's a difference between gloves and mitts. A baseball glove has fingers while a mitt doesn't. Only catchers and first basemen can wear a mitt.

First basemen are a key part of many plays so they need to be able to catch the ball easily.

GEAR AT BAT

Many players think batting gloves, which sometimes have a sticky palm, help them get a better grip on the bat. Another way of saying this is the gloves help create more friction so the batter has better control during their swing. Players also use batting gloves to prevent friction between the bat and their skin from creating blisters on their hands. Batting gloves became common in the 1980s. A batting helmet is a piece of equipment that has been mandatory, or required, since 1971. The hard plastic covering helps protect the head from wild pitches.

These larger mitts have more mass, though, which means it's harder to move them quickly. While more surface area is helpful for first basemen, quick movement is more important for many other players. This is why players at other positions use smaller gloves with less mass.

Catchers use different mitts. Catchers' mitts need to have a lot of padding. The edge of a catcher's mitt is thick, which helps catchers trap the ball after it hits their palm. Catchers' mitts need to be thick because of the force of the incoming ball.

Fast Fact

Catchers wear a lot of gear engineered especially to protect the body from the force of the pitches thrown at them. Their gear includes a mask, chest protector, and shin guards.

The harder the ball hits the catcher's mitt, the greater the force a catcher uses to stop it.

Infielders and outfielders use slightly different gloves too. Infielders' gloves are shallow for quicker throws, while outfielders' gloves are deeper for diving catches. Pitchers' gloves lack holes so the batter can't see what kind of grip a pitcher has on the ball (which could tell them what kind of pitch will be thrown).

Isaac Newton is sometimes called the father of physics. His laws of motion explain the world around us today, including sports.

NEWTON ENTERS THE GAME

Chapter Four

Isaac Newton was an English scientist who lived from 1643 to 1727—long before modern baseball came into existence. His three laws of motion describe the relationship between forces acting on an object and the object's motion. These laws of physics are easily applied to baseball.

Newton's Laws of Motion

Newton's first law states that an object at rest stays at rest and an object in motion stays in motion with the same speed and direction unless it's acted on by an outside force. A baseball resting on the ground will stay there until a player picks it up to throw it.

Newton's second law says the greater the mass of an object, the greater the force needed to make the object accelerate. A player needs to use more force to swing a baseball bat with more mass than a bat with less mass.

Newton's third law states that for every action, there's an equal and opposite **reaction**. When a ball hits a bat, it bounces off the bat with an equal amount of force.

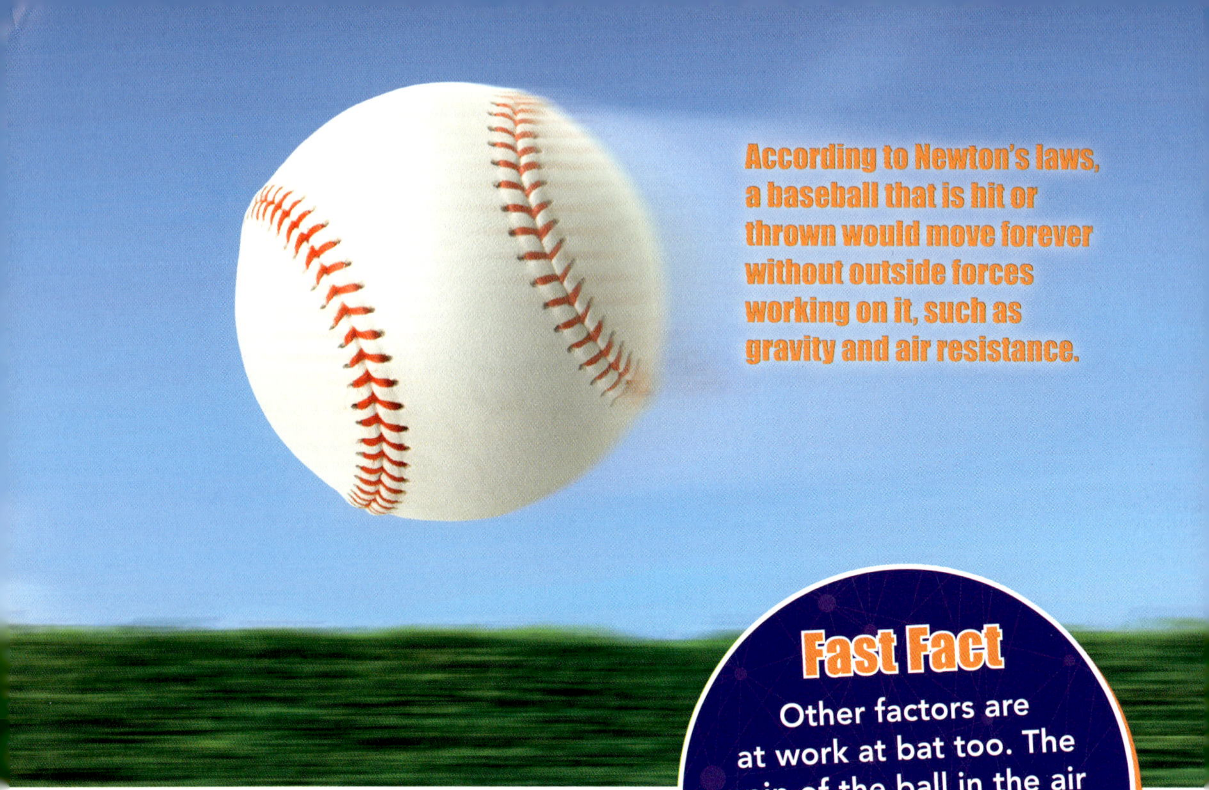

According to Newton's laws, a baseball that is hit or thrown would move forever without outside forces working on it, such as gravity and air resistance.

Fast Fact

Other factors are at work at bat too. The spin of the ball in the air can affect its speed and direction. Players also hold their bats at slightly different angles.

Energy at Work

Scientists used Newton's second law to prove that energy can't be created or destroyed. It only changes form. This is the law of **conservation** of energy.

The two main kinds of energy are on display in baseball: potential energy and kinetic energy. Potential energy is the amount of energy stored by an object when the object isn't using the energy. Kinetic energy is the energy that the object is using to do work.

When a pitcher holds a ball before a pitch, the ball has potential energy because it's not in motion. Once the ball is released, it has kinetic energy because it's moving toward the batter.

APPLYING THE THIRD LAW

Let's apply Newton's third law of motion to batting. Imagine two players swing their bats at the same speed, and they hit two baseballs with the exact same part of the bat. The first batter hits a fastball that's traveling 90 miles (145 km) per hour. The next batter hits one traveling 75 miles (121 km) per hour. The ball going faster will go farther. That ball hits the bat with more force, so it bounces off the bat with more force. The force of the reaction is equal to the force of the action.

If two hitters have the same bat speed, the one who hits a faster pitch will hit the ball farther.

The stops and starts of baseball provide many other examples of energy turning from potential to kinetic.

Fast Fact

When a player holds their bat high up before they swing it, the bat has potential energy. The swing changes the potential energy to kinetic energy.

Momentum and More

Newton's third law also explains why a player running to a base at top speed has a hard time stopping. Momentum is the quantity, or amount, of motion an object has. It can be found by multiplying an object's (or player's) mass by their velocity. The more momentum an object has, the harder it is to stop its motion. Professional baseball players generally have a lot of mass because they're big, strong athletes. They're also moving at a high velocity so they can get to the base before being out.

When you're in the middle of a baseball game, you're probably not thinking about Newton's laws and other STEM subjects. However, it's helpful—especially as a player—to remember your STEM. Knowledge of science, technology, engineering, and math can help you pitch that strike, catch that ball, and hit that home run!

Fast Fact

In baseball, a player can overrun first base and still be safe. They can't do that for second or third base, though.

Momentum can carry baserunners past second and third base, too, so they might slide to avoid being tagged out.

THINK ABOUT IT!

1. Do you agree that spitballs should be illegal? Why or why not?

2. Think of another way one of Newton's laws could be applied to baseball.

3. Would you recommend that athletes learn the STEM concepts behind their sports? Why or why not?

4. Do you think engineering and technology have made the game of baseball easier or harder than years ago? Why?

GLOSSARY

air pressure: The force exerted by air molecules on a surface.

conservation: The act of keeping a constant amount of something during a process of change.

decimal: A number that is between whole numbers and is written with a dot between its parts.

dimension: Length, width, height, or depth.

electromagnetic wave: A wave that carries energy produced when an electric field meets a magnetic field. Examples include visible light, radio waves, and X-rays.

formula: A general fact or rule in math often written using letters and symbols.

friction: A force that causes a moving object to slow down because it is in contact with another object.

humid: Having a high level of moisture, or water vapor, in the air.

pastime: An activity or hobby that someone does often for enjoyment rather than work.

professional: Having to do with a job someone does for a living.

reaction: The force that an object subjected to an outside force exerts in the opposite direction.

sphere: A round solid figure on which every point on its surface is an equal distance from its center.

technology: Using science, engineering, and other industries to invent useful tools or to solve problems. Also, a machine, piece of equipment, or method created by technology.

FIND OUT MORE

Books

Flynn, Brendan. *Baseball and Softball*. Minneapolis, MN: Early Encyclopedias, 2023.

Gigliotti, Jim. *Baseball: Score with STEM!* Minneapolis, MN: Bearport Publishing Company, 2022.

Ventura, Marne. *STEM in the World Series*. Minneapolis, MN: SportsZone, 2020.

Websites

How Baseball Works
www.howbaseballworks.com/TheBasics.htm
Brush up on your baseball basics here.

Science of Baseball
annex.exploratorium.edu/baseball/
Try these activities to learn more about the physics behind baseball.

Science of Baseball
www.mlb.com/mlb-youth-academy/science-of-baseball
This MLB website offers videos about baseball science.

Publisher's note to educators and parents: Our editors have carefully reviewed these websites to ensure that they are suitable for students. Many websites change frequently, however, and we cannot guarantee that a site's future contents will continue to meet our high standards of quality and educational value. Be advised that students should be closely supervised whenever they access the internet.

INDEX

LIFE WITH FOOD ALLERGIES

BY ANNETTE GULATI

The Child's World®
childsworld.com

Published by The Child's World®
1980 Lookout Drive • Mankato, MN 56003-1705
800-599-READ • www.childsworld.com

Content Consultant: Anna Nowak-Wegrzyn, M.D., Ph.D., Associate Professor of Pediatrics, Icahn School of Medicine at Mount Sinai

Photographs ©: Wave Break Media/Shutterstock Images, cover, 1; Shutterstock Images, 5 (top left), 12, 16; Virtu Studio/Shutterstock Images, 5 (top right); Gjoko Milovski/Shutterstock Images, 5 (bottom left); Hong Vo/Shutterstock Images, 5 (bottom right); Damir Cudic/iStockphoto, 6; Alexey Y. Petrov/Shutterstock Images, 8; iStockphoto, 10, 14; Anna Hoychuk/Shutterstock Images, 19; Pamela Joe McFarlane/ iStockphoto, 20

ISBN 9781503825123
LCCN 2017959680

Printed in the United States of America
PA02375

TABLE OF CONTENTS

FAST FACTS

- An allergy is a physical reaction to something. Some people have an allergic reaction when they eat, touch, or breathe in certain foods. The body thinks that the food is an invader, so the **immune system** tries to fight it off. Approximately 15 million Americans have food allergies, including nearly 6 million children.
- Symptoms can be mild, such as an itchy **rash**. Others are more serious. The most serious reaction is called **anaphylaxis**. Symptoms of anaphylaxis include vomiting and difficulty breathing.
- A person is at risk of developing food allergies if his or her family members have **asthma** or other allergies.
- There is no cure for food allergies. People with food allergies must avoid eating and being exposed to certain foods. They must also learn to spot their symptoms.
- **Antihistamines** can help manage symptoms. An **auto-injector** can be used to treat severe allergic reactions. The injector is filled with medicine called **epinephrine**. It is important to call an ambulance and get to a hospital if a serious reaction occurs.

TYPES OF FOOD ALLERGIES

Foods that commonly cause allergic reactions include peanuts, dairy, eggs, and tree nuts. The chart below shows the estimated percentages of US children with these types of food allergies.

Peanuts, 2–3%

Dairy, 1–2%

Eggs, 1.3%

Tree Nuts, 0.4–0.5%

Chapter 1

SARAH'S VACATION

Eleven-year-old Sarah and her parents boarded their airplane early. Right away, Sarah wiped down her seat and tray table with a disinfectant wipe. She wanted to make sure there were no traces of nuts anywhere.

Sarah tapped her feet on the floor. She had never been to Italy before. She couldn't wait. But she would have to be very careful. She was allergic to tree nuts. She couldn't eat almonds, hazelnuts, walnuts, or cashews.

Sarah's parents had ordered a special nut-free meal from the airline ahead of time. When they boarded, Sarah also told a flight attendant about her allergy.

◀ **People with food allergies pack food and medication when they travel.**

▲ **People with food allergies need to order special meals when they travel.**

Sarah asked the flight attendant to make an announcement so people wouldn't eat nuts around her. Sarah had also brought her own snacks.

Sarah checked to make sure she had remembered her auto-injector. Two years ago, she had accidentally eaten a cookie with walnuts in it. Her throat became itchy and swollen. Her mother injected the medicine into Sarah's thigh right away. It saved Sarah's life.

When Sarah and her family arrived in Italy, they were tired and hungry. The restaurant next to the hotel smelled wonderful. But Sarah was worried about eating out in a different country.

Before they left, Sarah's father had reminded her to bring her translation card. The card explained Sarah's tree nut allergy in Italian. Sarah showed the waiter the card. He told Sarah which meals were safe.

Sarah enjoyed her first meal in Italy. She was ready for the rest of her vacation.

TYPES OF NUT ALLERGIES

Tree nut and peanut allergies are both common types of allergies, but they are different. Tree nuts are nuts that grow on trees, including almonds, cashews, and hazelnuts. Peanuts grow as plants from the ground, so they are not tree nuts. Still, some people are allergic to both peanuts and tree nuts. Many foods that contain tree nuts are made on machines that also process peanuts. So people with any nut allergies need to read food labels carefully.

Chapter 2

LET'S EAT OUT

Twelve-year-old Kiara sat down with her friends, Jade and Maya. She picked up the restaurant menu. The smell of food made her stomach grumble. But Kiara's heart pounded. She had never gone out to a restaurant without her parents.

Kiara was allergic to seafood. She had to be careful selecting a restaurant and choosing her food. She remembered when she had found out about her allergy. After eating shrimp a few years ago, her skin had broken out in a rash. Her throat had tightened, and it became hard for her to breathe. An ambulance had brought her to an emergency room. She did not want that to happen again.

◂ **People who have food allergies need to read restaurant menus carefully and ask waitstaff lots of questions.**

At first, Kiara's friend Jade wanted to eat at a buffet restaurant. But Kiara knew that people often mixed up serving spoons. She told Jade there could be **cross-contamination**.

Maya suggested Chinese food. But Kiara knew that many Chinese dishes were made with oyster sauce or shrimp. There was risk of cross-contamination if cooking utensils were reused or not cleaned properly.

Finally, the girls found a restaurant. Kiara asked to speak with the manager.

ALLERGY DOCTORS

A special doctor called an allergist tests people for food allergies. The most common test is a skin prick test. A drop of solution is put on the patient's skin. The solution contains a particular food. Then the doctor pricks the skin to let the solution go in. Red, itchy, or swelling skin usually means the patient has an allergy to that food.

◀ **At buffet restaurants, food might mix and become contaminated.**

Kiara's doctor had told her that the best way to make sure she ate safe foods at a restaurant was to talk to the restaurant's chef or manager.

Kiara told the manager about her seafood allergy. She asked which meals might be safe for her to eat. The manager recommended a hamburger. But Kiara wasn't sure. *What if the seafood is cooked on the same grill as the hamburger?* she wondered. Kiara asked the manager. The manager told Kiara the grill was only used for meat. Kiara knew then that it was safe. But the French fries were cooked in the same oil as the fried shrimp. Instead, Kiara enjoyed a salad with her hamburger.

Kiara smiled and thanked the manager for her help. Eating at a restaurant was a lot of work. But Kiara was proud that she'd had a safe lunch out with her friends.

◂ **People with food allergies need to know how their food is cooked.**

Chapter 3

BIRTHDAY PARTY

Ryan watched his best friend, Luis, blow out ten birthday candles. Everyone clapped. Then Luis's sister handed Ryan a piece of birthday cake. Ryan thanked her but handed it back. He reminded her he was allergic to dairy and eggs. He couldn't eat the cake she'd offered because it had been made with those ingredients.

At first, Ryan had wondered if he should skip Luis's party this year. Sometimes his allergies made him feel left out. But he hadn't wanted to disappoint his best friend.

This was the first party Ryan had been to without his mother. Usually, she brought special food. She often stayed to make sure Ryan didn't eat something unsafe.

◀ **Many foods, such as cake, are often made with dairy and eggs.**

FOOD INTOLERANCES

A food intolerance is different from a food allergy. It is usually less serious. People with food intolerances are sensitive to certain foods and may have trouble digesting those foods. But they may be able to eat a small amount of the food without trouble. Lactose and gluten are two common food intolerances. Lactose is a type of sugar in milk, and gluten is a substance in wheat products such as bread.

This time, she hadn't been able to come. But Ryan had told everyone earlier about his food allergies, and he'd brought along dairy- and egg-free cupcakes. He'd also brought along his auto-injector just in case.

Ryan ate one of the dairy- and egg-free cupcakes he had brought. Everyone else wanted to try one, too. Ryan shared his special cupcakes.

Foods that normally have dairy or eggs can often be made without them.

At the end of the party, Luis gave out treat bags. Ryan knew he might not be able to eat the candies inside. He would have to read all the candy labels to see which ones contained dairy or eggs.

Ryan peeked inside the bag and smiled. Luis had given him little toys and baseball cards instead of candy. Ryan walked home happy and healthy. He couldn't wait to go to another birthday party.

THINK ABOUT IT

- What do you think would be the hardest part about having a food allergy?
- How is a person's life different if she or he has a food allergy?
- If you could invent something to help people with food allergies, what would it be?

◀ **People who have food allergies need to read ingredients labels closely.**

GLOSSARY

anaphylaxis (an-ah-fil-LAX-us): Anaphylaxis is a serious allergic reaction that occurs when a person's immune system releases a lot of chemicals, causing the person's blood pressure to drop quickly. Anaphylaxis can be life threatening if not treated right away.

antihistamines (an-tee-HYS-ta-meenz): Antihistamines are medicines used to treat colds and allergic reactions. A person with food allergies can take antihistamines to help reduce symptoms.

asthma (AZ-muh): Asthma is a condition that causes difficulty breathing and tightness in the chest. Many people with asthma also have food allergies.

auto-injector (AH-toh-in-JEKT-or): An auto-injector is a device used to inject medicine. An auto-injector is pressed into the thigh to release medicine.

cross-contamination (KRAWSS-kun-tam-ih-NAY-shun): Cross-contamination occurs when foods or substances get mixed. Cross-contamination can occur in restaurants or when many types of food are cooked in close proximity.

epinephrine (e-pin-EH-fryn): Epinephrine is a medicine used to fight severe allergic reactions. Auto-injectors are filled with epinephrine.

immune system (i-MYOON SISS-tuhm): The immune system is the part of a person's body that fights against infections and diseases. When a person's immune system thinks a certain type of food is an invader, it tries to protect the person from the food, causing an allergic reaction.

rash (RASH): A rash is an allergic reaction that causes a person's skin to break out in red, itchy spots. A rash is usually a mild symptom of an allergy.

TO LEARN MORE

Books

Boothroyd, Jennifer. *Caution in the Kitchen! Germs, Allergies, and Other Health Concerns*. Minneapolis, MN: Lerner, 2016.

Landau, Elaine. *Food Allergies*. Tarrytown, NY: Marshall Cavendish Benchmark, 2010.

Peters, Celeste A. *Food*. New York, NY: AV2 by Weigl, 2013.

Web Sites

Visit our Web site for links about food allergies:
childsworld.com/links

Note to Parents, Teachers, and Librarians: We routinely verify our Web links to make sure they are safe and active sites. So encourage your readers to check them out!

SELECTED BIBLIOGRAPHY

"Food Allergy." *American College of Asthma, Allergy & Immunology*. American College of Asthma, Allergy & Immunology, 2014. Web. 7 Nov. 2017.

"Food Allergy 101." *Food Allergy Research & Education*. Food Allergy Research & Education, n.d. Web. 7 Nov. 2017.

"Living with Food Allergies." *Kids with Food Allergies*. Asthma and Allergy Foundation of America, n.d. Web. 7 Nov. 2017.

Miller, Sloane. *Allergic Girl: Adventures in Living Well with Food Allergies*. Wiley, 2011. Print.

INDEX

ABOUT THE AUTHOR

Annette Gulati is the author of five nonfiction books for children. She also writes stories, articles, poems, crafts, and activities for magazines and educational publishers. She lives in Seattle, Washington, with her family.